THERE WAS AN OLD PIRATE WHO SWALLOWED A FISH

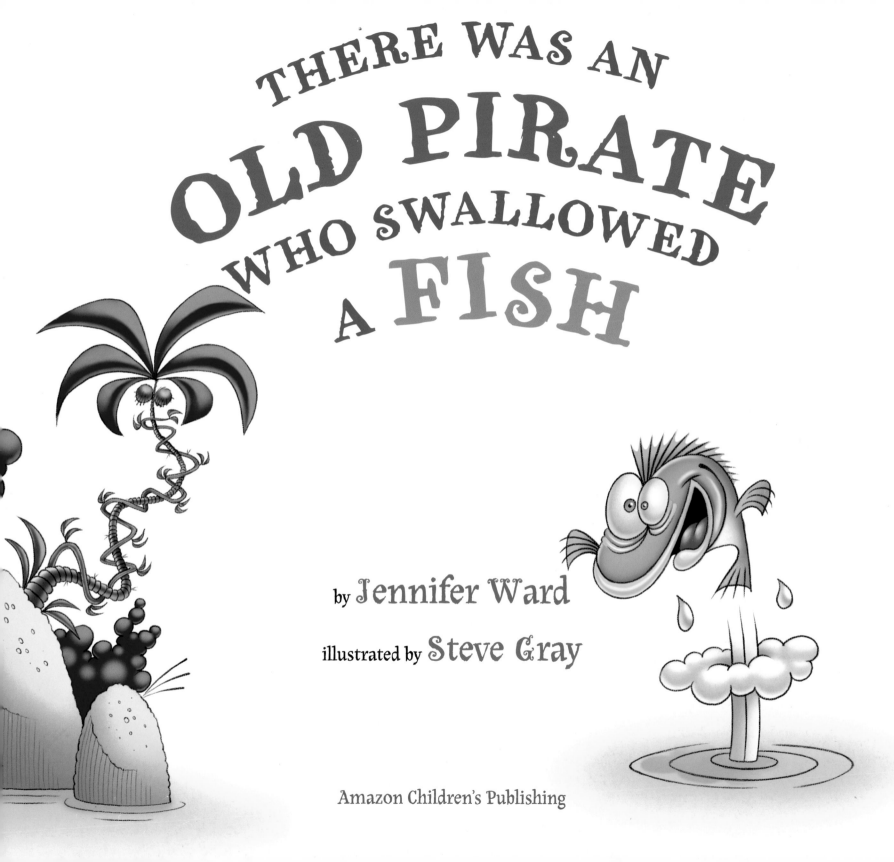

by **Jennifer Ward**

illustrated by **Steve Gray**

Amazon Children's Publishing

Text copyright © 2012 by Jennifer Ward
Illustrations copyright © 2012 by Steve Gray

All rights reserved
Amazon Publishing
Attn: Amazon Children's Books
P.O. Box 400818
Las Vegas, NV 89149
www.amazon.com/amazonchildrenspublishing

Library of Congress Cataloging-in-Publication Data
Ward, Jennifer, 1963-
There was an old pirate who swallowed a fish / by Jennifer Ward ;
illustrated by Steve Gray. — 1st ed.
p. cm.
Summary: This variation on the traditional, cumulative rhyme
looks at the consequences of a pirate's strange diet.
ISBN 978-0-7614-6196-8 (hardcover) — ISBN 978-0-7614-6197-5 (ebook)
1. Folk songs, English—England—Texts. [1. Folk songs. 2. Nonsense verses.]
I. Gray, Steve, 1950- ill. II. Little old lady who swallowed a fly. III. Title.
PZ8.3.W2135Tht 2012
782.42—dc23
[E]
2011036695

The illustrations are rendered in digital media.
Book design by Vera Soki
Editor: Marilyn Brigham

Printed in China (W)
First edition
10 9 8 7 6 5 4 3 2 1

To Miss M., who loves books as much as I do
—J. W.

To my wench, Cindy. You be this pirate's treasure!
—S. G.

THERE WAS AN OLD PIRATE . . . .

. . . who swallowed a *fish*.

With a swoosh and a swish, down went that fish.
Blimey! But that fish was slimy!
Why did he swallow it? I don't know.
Yo ho ho! Watch his belly grow!

There was an old pirate who swallowed a *bird*.

How absurd! He swallowed a bird!
He swallowed the bird right after the fish.
Blimey! But that fish was slimy!
Why did he swallow it? I don't know.
Yo ho ho! Watch his belly grow!

Thud!

There was an old pirate who swallowed a *map*.

With a flip and a flap, it went down in a snap.
He swallowed the map right after the bird.
He swallowed the bird right after the fish.
Blimey! But that fish was slimy!
Why did he swallow it? I don't know.

Yo ho ho! Watch his belly grow!

There was an old pirate . . .

...who swallowed some *gold*.

He plundered, I'm told, then swallowed that gold.
He swallowed the gold right after the map.
He swallowed the map right after the bird.
He swallowed the bird right after the fish.
Blimey! But that fish was slimy!
Why did he swallow it? I don't know.
Yo ho ho! Watch his belly grow!

There was an old pirate
who swallowed a *chest*.

He loved it best, that treasure-filled chest.
He swallowed the chest right after the gold.
He swallowed the gold right after the map.
He swallowed the map right after the bird.
He swallowed the bird right after the fish.
Blimey! But that fish was slimy!
Why did he swallow it? I don't know.

Yo ho ho! Watch his belly grow!

There was an old pirate who swallowed a *plank*.
He walked that plank, then gave it a yank.

He swallowed the plank right after the chest.
He swallowed the chest right after the gold.
He swallowed the gold right after the map.
He swallowed the map right after the bird.
He swallowed the bird right after the fish.
Blimey! But that fish was slimy!
Why did he swallow it? I don't know.
Yo ho ho! Watch his belly grow!

There was an old pirate . . .

. . . who swallowed a *sail*.
A grand, old sail, as big as a whale.

He swallowed the sail right after the plank.
He swallowed the plank right after the chest.
He swallowed the chest right after the gold.
He swallowed the gold right after the map.
He swallowed the map right after the bird.
He swallowed the bird right after the fish.
Blimey! But that fish was slimy!
Why did he swallow it? I don't know.

Yo ho ho! Watch his belly grow!

There was an old pirate . . .

. . . who swallowed a *mast*.

It went down fast, that wooden mast.
He swallowed the mast right after the sail.
He swallowed the sail right after the plank.
He swallowed the plank right after the chest.
He swallowed the chest right after the gold.
He swallowed the gold right after the map.
He swallowed the map right after the bird.
He swallowed the bird right after the fish.
Blimey! But that fish was slimy!
Why did he swallow it? I don't know.

Yo ho ho! Watch his belly grow!

There was an old pirate who swallowed a *ship*.

With a grip and a flip, down went the ship.
He swallowed the ship right after the mast.
He swallowed the mast right after the sail.
He swallowed the sail right after the plank.
He swallowed the plank right after the chest.
He swallowed the chest right after the gold.
He swallowed the gold right after the map.
He swallowed the map right after the bird.
He swallowed the bird right after the fish.
Blimey! But that fish was slimy!
Why did he swallow it? I don't know.

Yo ho ho! Watch his belly grow!

There was an old pirate, a captain he be,
who sunk to the bottom of the deep,

dark . . .